Helena Clare Pittman ONCE
WHEN I WAS SCARED

illustrated by Ted Rand

A PUFFIN
UNICORN

When Grandfather was a boy and lived upstate in the mountains, his mother sent him to get hot coals from the neighbors next door. Next door was across two hills and through a dark wood.

The stove had gone out, and dank air now seeped through the walls of the cabin. After a week of steady autumn drizzle, the woodpile was too damp to kindle coal.

Grandfather's mother took the tin box with the wooden handle down from the shelf.

"Don't go wandering, Daniel," she said as she looked uneasily through the curtains at the sky. "It feels like a storm is coming."

Daniel pushed his feet into his boots and put on his coat.

Then he picked up the box,
stepped outside, and headed
toward the woods.

A few fiery autumn leaves still
clung to the trees, the only bright
color in the foggy valley. They
shivered in the wind, which stung
Daniel's cheeks.

"Hurry back!" his mother
called. "It will be dark soon."

But her voice sounded far away. Daniel was already sliding, half falling through the wet leaves, down the far side of the first hill. The wind blew smoky-looking clouds across the sky and whistled through the holes in the sides of the coal box. Daniel stumbled over slippery rocks and roots as he tried to run. Tangles of branches caught his woolen leggings, slowing him.

But suddenly he broke free.
Now he moved easily over the
roots, springing gracefully off
rocks with his strong back legs.
His sharp claws dug into the
leaves. Behind him a silvery
tail bounced on the wind, its
white tip a bright flicker in
the shadows.

Then he was knocking at the Nickersons' door, his heart pounding.

"Come in, Daniel," Mrs. Nickerson said with a friendly smile. "Catch your breath and warm yourself."

"Mama is waiting," he panted. "May I have some coals? Our fire went out."

Mrs. Nickerson filled his tin box with coals from the stove and snapped the lid shut. The box felt warm in his hands as she rewrapped his muffler snugly under his chin.

"Good night, Daniel," she called as he left the clearing.

In the dark wood, Daniel started
to run. Soon he was covered with
sweat underneath his warm clothes.
An owl hooted in a tree above him.
As he looked up, something caught
his foot and he fell. He struggled
to free himself but it wrapped more
tightly around his legs. In the
shadows it looked like a snake.

Gripping the box, he twisted over
like a cat. A big cat. A bobcat.

In a second he bounded away,
free. His balance was sure. He was
long and lithe. His paws made no
sound as he leaped again and again
over the fallwood and underbrush.

He could see the hill behind
his house, when suddenly he heard
a crash of branches. Ahead was a
huge black shape. It looked like
a bear, crouching. The fur on its
neck stood straight up. He heard
it snarl. A bear stood between him
and home.

In the place of his cat's paws were
his leather boots and mittened hands.
Shaking, he dropped the tin box.
The lid fell open and coals scattered,
hissing on the wet ground.

The bear turned and rose on
its back legs. Daniel jumped
back. He felt himself rise off
the ground. His feet became
talons, his arms huge dark
wings that lifted him up above
the bear. He shouted at the
top of his voice to frighten it.
The sound that came from
his throat was the shriek of
an eagle.

The bear lumbered off into the woods. Moonlight flickered through churning clouds as the great bird landed in the leaves.

Daniel took a long, deep breath, then looked at himself. His wings were gone. He was wearing his coat, which was matted with dirt, and his muffler was still wound around his neck.

Then he knelt and put the glowing coals back into the tin box. He brushed off his clothes, picked up the box, and climbed the hill.

Rain was just beginning to fall as he reached home.

"How quickly you went
and came, Daniel," said his
mother. She held him close.
Her warmth felt good against
his cheek. "Hardly fifteen
minutes passed since you left!"
   She took the coals and
laid a bed in the stove for the
kindling. Flames soon danced
through the crackling twigs.

"Did it really happen, Grandfather?" I asked.

"I found these in my coat the next day," answered my grandfather. He held out two stiff pinion feathers. By their markings they could only have come from an eagle.

He gave them to me, once when I was scared. I put those feathers in my drawer, where I still keep them. Sometimes, when I feel afraid, I take them out. I hold them in my fingers and remember the look in my grandfather's eyes when he gave them to me.

To Albert V. Jessen,
who gave me a feather to keep
H.C.P.

To my son, Martin,
the boy in the forest
T.R.

PUFFIN UNICORN BOOKS

Published by the Penguin Group
Penguin Books USA Inc., 375 Hudson Street,
New York, New York 10014, U.S.A.
Penguin Books Ltd, 27 Wrights Lane,
London W8 5TZ, England
Penguin Books Australia Ltd, Ringwood,
Victoria, Australia
Penguin Books Canada Ltd, 10 Alcorn Avenue,
Toronto, Ontario, Canada M4V 3B2
Penguin Books (N.Z.) Ltd, 182-190 Wairau Road,
Auckland 10, New Zealand
Penguin Books Ltd, Registered Offices:
Harmondsworth, Middlesex, England

Text copyright © 1988 by Helena Clare Pittman
Illustrations copyright © 1988 by Ted Rand
All rights reserved.
Unicorn is a registered trademark of
Dutton Children's Books,
a division of Penguin Books USA Inc.

Library of Congress number 88-3598
ISBN 0-14-054932-3

Published in the United States by
Dutton Children's Books,
a division of Penguin Books USA Inc.
Designer: Barbara Powderly
Printed in Hong Kong by South China Printing Co.
First Puffin Unicorn Edition 1993
10 9 8 7 6 5 4 3 2 1

ONCE WHEN I WAS SCARED is also available
in hardcover from Dutton Children's Books.